UNEXPECTED FRIENDS

By **Tim Welch**

Illustrated by **Katie Simpson**

First Published by AM Ink Publishing LLC, Southwick, MA

www.AMInkPublishing.com

I want to dedicate this book to, my wife Emily, my heart, my soul, my best friend, someone who has stood by me in this journey, and has always been my shoulder to lean on. I love you with all my heart and soul. To my daughter Mercedes, you have always been my angel, you saved me and was there for me when no one else was, daddy loves you. To my son Nixon, I see so much of me in you and want you to see what can happen if you reach for your dreams, daddy loves you bug. And to my mom Leslie, you came into my life when I needed you the most, I never knew the love of a mother until you came into my life, I can never thank you enough. I love you all so much! A very special thanks to Eileen Dietz for all of your help.

This book was created based on things I went through growing up. After my accident I became a target, I was bullied horribly, kids don't see the damage they can cause by just one single word. I want the message that if this was you going through this, could you handle it? I hope this book can help stop at least one person from being bullied.

Timmy always watched the other kids play from a distance.

Timmy wasn't like the other kids, Timmy was in a wheelchair.

He watched them run, skip, jump, play ball, things Timmy wished he could do, but knew he couldn't.

1

Even if they would just ask him to join them, to let him feel like he was part of the others. But Timmy had no friends, everyone treated him differently because of his disability. All he wanted was to be treated the same as the other kids.

At school, there was always a group of kids that bullied Timmy. They made fun of him, they pushed him, they teased him, not caring about his feelings.

Every time Timmy would tell an adult about what was going on, they just told him, "Just ignore them," not knowing how bad it really was.

He was treated the same way at home as he was at school. It was like no one would listen to him.

One day at school, the teacher told the students that one of their classmates had been hurt real bad in an accident. This made all of the kids very sad.

6

Then the teacher told the students who the student was that got hurt. It was Billy, one of the kids that Bullied Timmy in school. Even though Billy was so mean to Timmy, he still felt sad that Billy got hurt. He didn't want to see anyone hurt.

After time, Billy came back to school but Billy was now in a wheel chair. The one thing that Billy noticed was that his friends were not his friends anymore, and that the other kids were making fun of him. This really hurt Billy.

The whole time, Timmy was watching from a distance, watching how everyone treated Billy.

Timmy knew exactly how Billy felt, sad and alone. One day at the playground, Timmy noticed

Billy alone and crying. So he approached him.

"What's wrong Billy?" Timmy asked.

Billy said, "No one likes me anymore because

I'm different."

Timmy said, "Kind of like how you treated me?"

Billy looked at Timmy and started to cry.

"I'm so sorry, I never looked at it that way," said Billy, with tears in his eyes.

Then Billy turned around and started to wheel away in his wheelchair, with his head hung low. 11

Timmy said, "Where are you going?"

Billy replied, "Away! Just please know that
I am truly sorry for hurting you."

Timmy raised his hand and said, "Wait!"

Timmy continued, "No, please stay, just because of what happened in the past, doesn't mean we can't be friends. You now understand how I felt and you see how bad it hurts, we can be friends."

Billy's face lit up with a smile.

"Really?" Billy replied.

"You now know how it feels to be treated differently, and it hurts. You don't have to just hit someone for it to hurt, words and actions hurt too. Just because someone is different on the outside does not mean they are different on the inside." Timmy said.

15

As the boys talked about their injuries Billy told Timmy that his time in the wheelchair was limited and eventually he would walk again.

This made Timmy very happy to hear but also afraid that things would go back to the way they were before Billy's accident. Timmy felt that he was losing the only person that understood him.

Billy came back to school, no wheelchair, his casts gone. Before you knew it Billy's friends were back by his side, like nothing ever happened.

Soon after, Billy notice his friends picking on Timmy. Billy saw Timmy in tears and this upset him.

"STOP!" Billy yelled. "You did this to me when I was hurt, I know how it feels and I didn't like it!" This made Billy's friends think about what they had done and they felt terrible.

Timmy was so happy that Billy stood up for him. He finally had a true friend.

Timmy finally got what he always wanted.

Friends that understood him.

THE END

To my mom, dad and the rest of my family for supporting and

encouraging my art.

And a special thanks to my dad who always told me to...

"Just keep doing what you're doing!"

And

Mrs. Jennifer Fowler for teaching me that my disability was

NOT a disability.

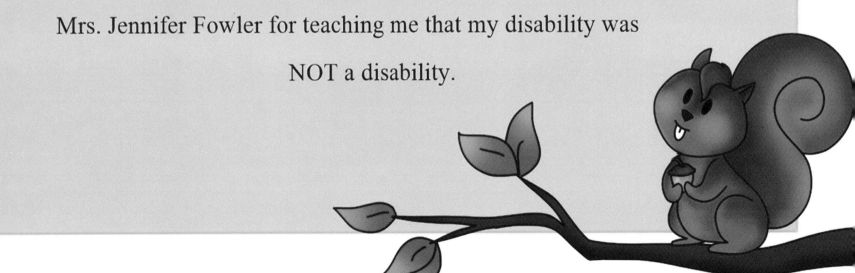

CPSIA information can be obtained at www.ICGtesting.com
Printed in the USA
LVIW011911041119
636236LV00003B/58